Mythical Creatures' Legendary Histories: Haiku A to Z

Copyright © 2018 Travis M. Blair
Text: Travis M. Blair
Illustration: David Buist

All rights reserved. This book or any portion thereof may not be reproduced or used in any manner whatsoever without the express written permission of the publisher except for the use of brief quotations in a book review.

Untold Tales of Bigfoot and Related Characters © Vince Dorse
Editor: Amy Waeschle

ISBN: 978-1-7326982-1-5

Published by Zarfling Platoon
info@zarfling.com
zarfling.com

> "Hey, you know who we should get to write the foreword on mythological creatures and their relevance to modern society? The guy who draws that Bigfoot comic!"
> "Brilliant idea! That'll add an extra level of class and legitimacy to the book!"

This is a conversation that *probably* never happened. Though, I like to pretend it happened because it makes me feel good. Just a little myth I choose to believe in.

But I think the reason I got this gig — aside from the fact that I work cheap — is because what I'm doing with my Bigfoot comic is the same thing the creators of this book are doing. The same thing thousands of people around the world have been doing for ages. We're employing creatures of myth in creative ways to help us tell stories and entertain. It's actually an ancient tradition.

Myths, and the creatures that spring from them, are some of the more colorful cornerstones around which people build their cultures and societies. That may sound lofty but, really, these are the heroes and monsters we use to tell stories, teach lessons, and administer warnings. Ancient Greeks told tales of Heracles to celebrate unrivaled strength while condemning unbridled anger. Mermaid lore was started by early sailors, their stories intended as both fantasy fulfillment and cautionary tales against slipshod ship steering.

The reason these stories work so well is that some of these creatures are very easy to believe in. Some of them we want to believe in. The Loch Ness Monster. Mermaids. Werewolves. And what about Bigfoot? It isn't difficult to imagine that somewhere, solitary in his hidden lair, there exists a lumbering beast with giant feet who shuns mankind. There's literally someone matching that description typing this foreword. And there are very simple reasons we want to believe in these mythical creatures. One is that it's nice to imagine there's still mystery in the world. Something magical and apart from us. But the flip side of that is also compelling. We can believe some of these creatures exist because we see in them the best and worst parts of our own human nature.

We all have the potential within us to act upon our vices or our virtues, and the tales of these mythological beasts can offer a clue as to how either choice might play out in the real world. That's the reason myths never die. We're not really telling stories about gods and monsters. We're telling stories about ourselves. About the human condition. After all this time we're still trying to figure out how this stuff works. Maybe if we keep telling these stories, we can actually affect change. Make things better. Maybe. I like to pretend that could happen, anyway. It's just a little myth I choose to believe in.

- Vince Dorse

Creator of Untold Tales of Bigfoot
October, 2017

What's a haiku?

Haiku is a type of poetry from Japan that has become popular around the world! Haiku poems are short and descriptive. They connect the reader to an element of nature.

Traditional haiku written in English consists of 3 lines and 17 syllables.

First line is 5 syllables
Second line is 7 syllables
Third line is 5 syllables

Japanese writers have been creating haiku for centuries! Haiku is formal, with rules about content and structure.

Because of the differences between Japanese and English grammar, the way this form of poetry is written has changed over time. Rules have been broken! The mythical creatures haiku in this book do not follow every rule either! Though we did obey to the 5/7/5 structure. Enjoy!

ALPHYN

From times medieval
Lion and wolf, knotted tail
Seen on heraldry

BANSHEE

Long, disheveled hair
She wails about the deceased
A ghost with foresight

CENTAUR

Tribal warriors
Galloped upon ancient lands
Of both man and horse

DWARF

Stout and strong, persists
Defending the tall mountain
Against mighty odds

ELF
Sweet and graceful, they Residing within forest At one with nature

FAUNESS

Half woman, half goat
Similar to satyress
Rare classical art

GOBLIN

Out of the dark caves
Diminutive and mean, they
Greedy for treasure

HARPY
Large bird, woman's face
Swooping to snatch people, food
Known as hounds of Zeus

IMP

So mischievous
Pair of wings and small clawed toes
A huddle of scamps

JINN

Hidden, made like clouds
Created from smokeless flame
They are of three types

KRAKEN

Giant sea creature
Overtaking ship and crew
Tentacles snap mast

LEPRECHAUN

Shoemaker trickster
Water spirit and fairy
Wore red before green

MANTICORE

A hybrid creature
Lion body, human head
Shark teeth and bat wings

NAGA

Serpentine person
Guardians of shining gems
Underground kingdom

OGRE

Grotesque cannibal
Hairy, with big head and mouth
Such strength and hunger

PIXIE

Dance outdoors all night!
Fluttering wings, pointed ears
At odds with fairies

QUINOTAUR

The beast of Neptune
From a page of dynasty
Horned crown upon head

ROC

Giant bird of prey
Feasts upon an elephant
Mountain in the air

TANIWHA

From caves in rivers
Large, shape-shifting sea creatures
Tribal guardians

VALKYRIE

Chooser of the slain
Soaring over battlefields
Building an army

WEREWOLF

Man among others
Becomes wolf under full moon
Afflicted savage

XING TIAN

Head buried and lost
Returning with ambition
Brandishing again

YETI

Abominable
Glacier being, wild man
Prints left in the snow

ZOMBIE

Dead, yet is alive!
An insatiable hunger
Bites make more undead

What type of mythical creature would you make?

Would it live in the mountains or live in a lake?

Would it have wings, and be short and small?

Would it have horns, and tower over all?

Would the creature have a unique feature?

Just how would you make this creature?

Made in the USA
San Bernardino, CA
03 June 2019